THE
LITTLE GIRL
AND
THE DRAGON

BY Else Holmelund Minarik

PICTURES BY

Martine Gourbault

Greenwillow Books, New York

Text copyright © 1991 by Else Minarik Bigart
Illustrations copyright © 1991 by Martine Gourbault
All rights reserved. No part of this book
may be reproduced or utilized in any form
or by any means, electronic or mechanical,
including photocopying, recording, or by
any information storage and retrieval
system, without permission in writing
from the Publisher, Greenwillow Books,
a division of William Morrow & Company, Inc.,
1350 Avenue of the Americas, New York, NY 10019.
Printed in Hong Kong by South China
Printing Company (1988) Ltd.
First Edition 10 9 8 7 6 5 4 3 2 1

Library of Congress Cataloging-in-Publication Data

Minarik, Else Holmelund.
The little girl and the dragon / by Else Holmelund Minarik;
pictures by Martine Gourbault.
p.   cm.
Summary: A dragon escapes from a storybook and proceeds to
swallow up all of a little girl's toys.
ISBN 0-688-09913-0 (trade) ISBN 0-688-09914-9 (lib.)
[1. Dragons—Fiction.   2. Behavior—Fiction.]
I. Gourbault, Martine, ill.   II. Title.
PZ7.M652Lk   1991
[E]—dc20   90-38495   CIP   AC

For Mandy
—E. H. M.

For Sacha
—M. G.

Once there was a little girl
who had a book about a dragon.

One day the dragon got out of the book.

He swallowed
her stuffed dog and
her baby doll and
her doll's bed
and the doll carriage.

And then he swallowed her minicomputer
and her best game and her cash register

and all her puzzles.

He also swallowed her doll house.

"Now, that's enough!" said the little girl.

"I want all those things back,

and right away, too!"

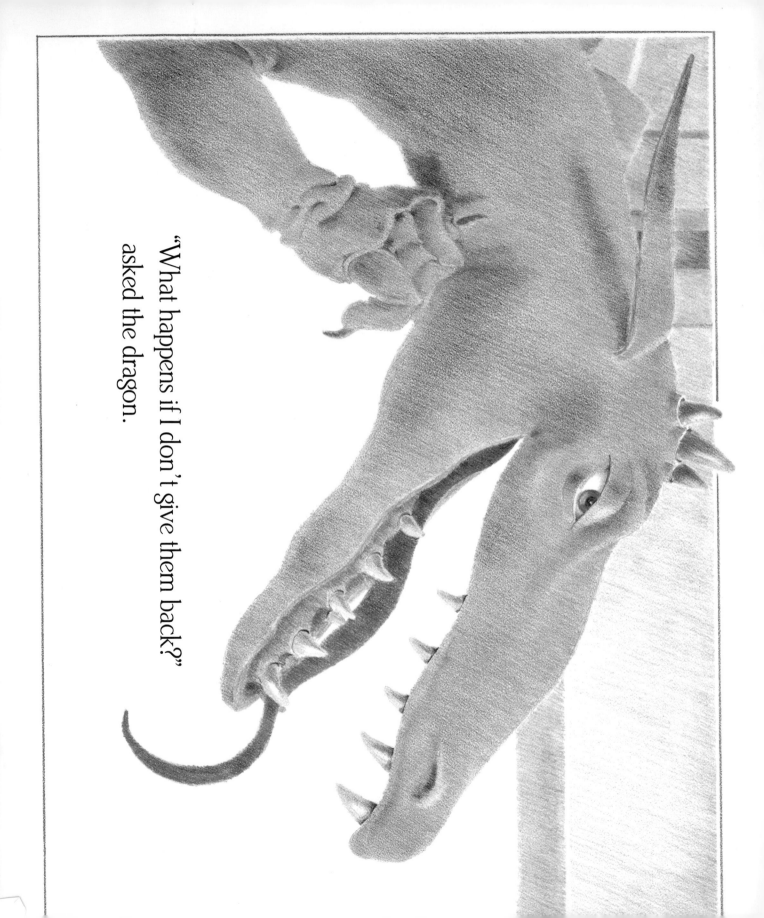

"What happens if I don't give them back?" asked the dragon.

"Why, I'll sit on this book, and you'll have no place to stay," said the little girl.

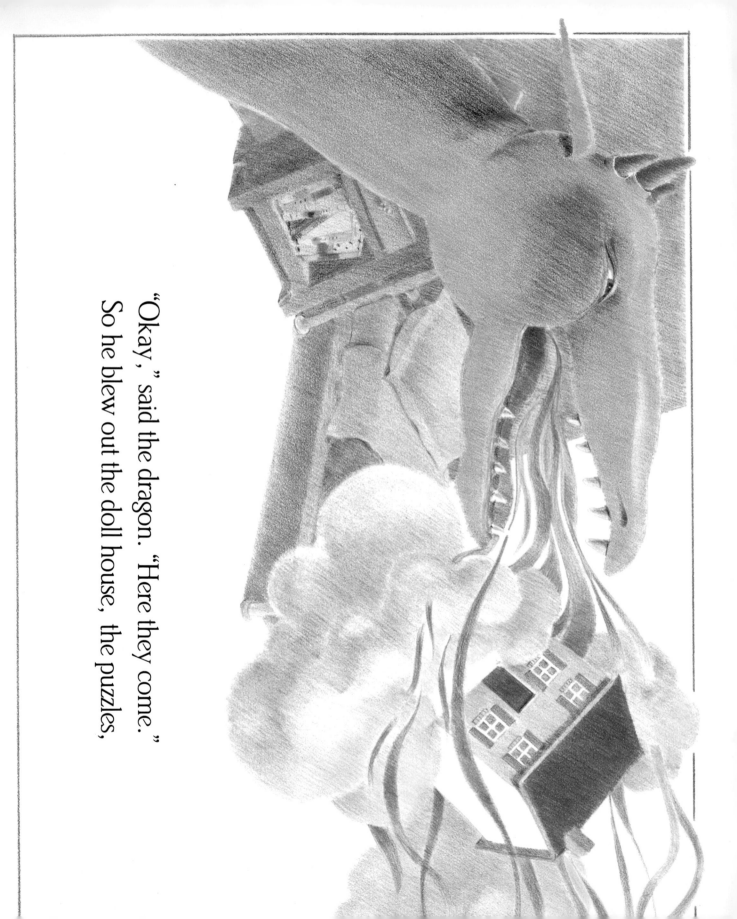

"Okay," said the dragon. "Here they come."
So he blew out the doll house, the puzzles,

the cash register, the best game,
and the minicomputer.

And then he blew out
the doll carriage, the doll's bed,

and the baby doll.

"One more thing," said the little girl.
"I want my stuffed dog, too."

"Can't I keep it?"
asked the dragon.
"No!" said the little girl.

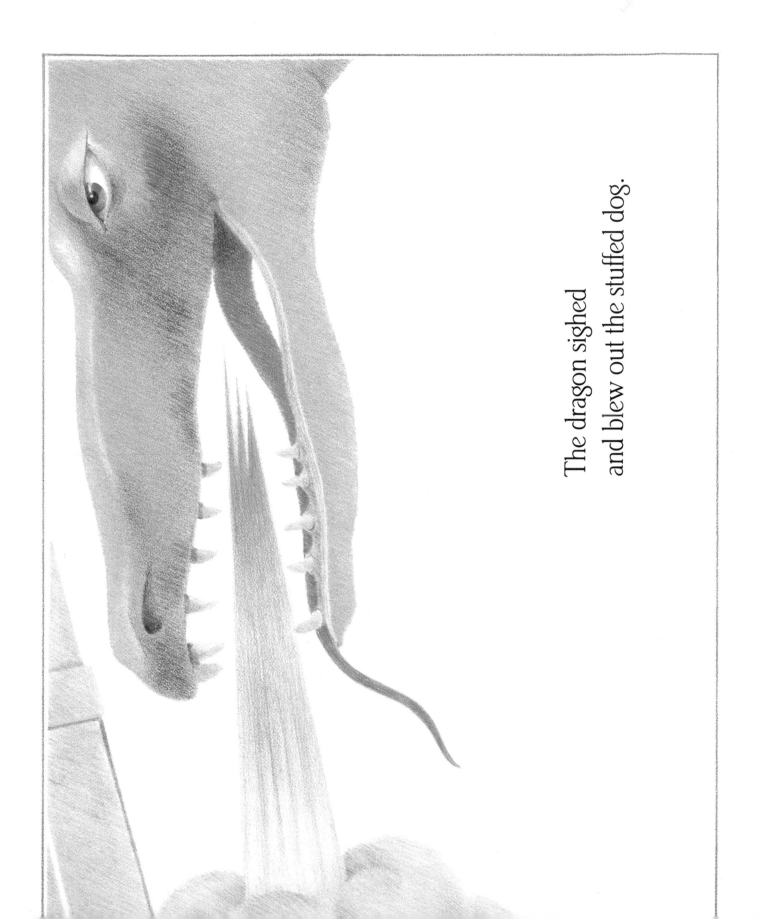

The dragon sighed
and blew out the stuffed dog.

And then the little girl
let him back in the book—

where he belonged.